Clara
the Chocolate
Fairy

Special thanks to
Narinder Dhami

ORCHARD BOOKS
338 Euston Road, London NW1 3BH
Orchard Books Australia
Level 17/207 Kent Street, Sydney, NSW 2000
A Paperback Original

First published in 2013 by Orchard Books

Illustrations © Orchard Books 2013

A CIP catalogue record for this book is available
from the British Library.

ISBN 978 1 40832 499 8

1 3 5 7 9 10 8 6 4 2

Printed in Great Britain

The paper and board used in this paperback are natural recyclable
products made from wood grown in sustainable forests. The
manufacturing processes conform to the environmental regulations
of the country of origin.

Orchard Books is a division of Hachette Children's Books,
an Hachette UK company

www.hachette.co.uk

Clara
the Chocolate
Fairy

by Daisy Meadows

ORCHARD

www.rainbowmagic.co.uk

Jack Frost's Spell

I have a plan to cause some strife
And use those fairies to change my life.
I'm going to take their charms away
And make my dreams come true today!

I'll build a castle made of sweets,
And spoil the fairies' silly treats.
I just don't care how much they whine,
Their cakes and lollies will be mine!

Contents

Chocolate Crisis

"I'm *so* looking forward to this!' Rachel Walker told her best friend, Kirsty Tate, her voice brimming over with excitement. The two girls were walking up one of the hills that overlooked Wetherbury village. "I've never been to a sweet factory before. I can't wait to see inside *Candy Land.*"

"Me, too," Kirsty agreed happily.

"Wasn't it kind of Aunt Harri to arrange a tour of the factory for my birthday treat?" Kirsty's aunt worked at *Candy Land* in the cookie department.

"Yes, and it isn't your birthday until tomorrow, so it's almost like having an *extra* treat!" Rachel pointed out as they climbed higher up the hill.

Ahead of them they could see the sweet factory with the big pink-and-white *Candy Land* sign over the wrought-iron gates. "Do you think we might get to try a few sweets while we're on the tour?" Rachel added eagerly.

Kirsty grinned. "I hope so!" she replied.

"I'm really looking forward to seeing the chocolates being made. My favourite is the Sticky Toffo Choc — it's gorgeous, sticky toffee covered with yummy chocolate!" But then Kirsty's smile faded. "Remember, though, Rachel," she went on, "some of the sweets might not taste very nice, now that Jack Frost and his goblins have the Sweet Fairies' magic charms."

Rachel nodded solemnly. Yesterday, just after she'd arrived to spend the half-term holiday with Kirsty, their old friend Honey the Sweet Fairy had appeared to whisk the girls off to Fairyland. There the girls had met Honey's helpers, the seven Sweet Fairies who look after all the delicious, mouth-watering sweets in both Fairyland and the human world.

11

Rachel and Kirsty were very upset when they discovered that Jack Frost and his goblins had stolen the Sweet Fairies' magical objects. But they couldn't believe it when they found out exactly *why* Jack Frost needed the magical charms. It was because he'd ordered his goblins to build him a castle made entirely of sweets!

To make things worse, King Oberon and Queen Titania had explained to the girls that Treat Day, a special Fairyland festival, was coming up very soon. On Treat Day, the king and queen gave each fairy throughout the land a basket full of sweets, but this year there wouldn't be any treat baskets at all if the magic charms weren't quickly returned to the Sweet Fairies. Jack Frost had given

the seven charms to his goblins to keep
safe in the human world, and Rachel
and Kirsty had promised to help their
fairy friends to find them. Then sweets
everywhere would taste delicious again,
and Treat Day wouldn't be ruined for all
the fairies.

"It's not just my birthday tomorrow,"
Kirsty said, "It's Treat Day in Fairyland,
too! We *must* find the missing magical
charms before then, Rachel."

Rachel nodded.

"Three down, four
to go!" she said
with a smile.
"We're going
to find them all,
Kirsty – I just
know it!"

13

"I wonder if we'll see one of our fairy friends at *Candy Land* today?" Kirsty remarked. "Or maybe Jack Frost and his goblins will be there, too."

"We'll be ready for him!" Rachel replied. "Look, isn't that Aunt Harri waiting for us under the *Candy Land* sign?"

Aunt Harri waved as Rachel and Kirsty hurried towards the factory gates.

"You're right on time, girls," she greeted them with a smile. "Come along, I'll take you to the reception area where the rest of the tour group are waiting for you. Are you looking forward to seeing the factory?"

"Oh, YES!" Kirsty and Rachel chorused. Aunt Harri laughed. She led the girls through the gates to a door with RECEPTION printed on it. Inside the office were several people waiting for the tour, including an elderly couple and several families with young children.

The first thing Kirsty noticed when they entered the reception area was the wonderful, sweet, sugary smell.

She breathed in deeply and then smiled when she saw Rachel doing exactly the same.

"Girls, I have to rush off back to the cookie department," Aunt Harri told them. "One of the guides, Matt, will show you around, and I'll meet you in the canteen later for lunch."

"Thanks, Aunt Harri," Kirsty replied.

A few moments after Aunt Harri left, a tall young man wearing a snow-white apron and hat bounced into the office.

"Welcome to *Candy Land*!" he announced, beaming at everyone. "I'm Matt, your tour guide today. I'm going to explain how our fabulous, mouth-watering sweets are made, and you'll get the chance to try some of them, too."

The girls exchanged delighted glances.
"This way to the tasting room!" Matt
went on, opening a door on the other
side of the office. Everyone filed through
into a brightly coloured room that had
walls painted with bright pink-and-white
stripes. On a table in the middle of the
room, laid out on trays, were sparkly
pink-and-white gift boxes filled with
delicious-looking chocolates.

"Look, Sticky Toffo Choc!" Rachel murmured, pointing out the label on one of the boxes to Kirsty.

"Please help yourselves," Matt told them. "Then we'll go into the factory, and you can find out exactly how your favourite chocolates are made."

Everyone gathered around the table. Kirsty selected a Sticky Toffo Choc and eagerly popped it into her mouth. But the bitterness of the chocolate immediately made her gasp in disgust. It tasted *terrible*!

Rachel had chosen Golden Crunch, a star-shaped chocolate filled with honeycomb. But like Kirsty, she also got a shock when she tasted it.

"This is horrible!" Rachel murmured to Kirsty, trying to swallow down the bitter chocolate as fast as possible. "It's the worst chocolate I've ever had!"

Kirsty glanced around the tasting room. The other tour members were looking very unimpressed with the chocolates, too. The elderly couple were pulling faces at each other, and one of the small children burst into tears.

"Nasty chocolate, Mummy!" she wailed.

Matt was looking flustered. "Oh dear, I don't know what's gone wrong today!" he said apologetically. "The chocolate-tasting is usually a highlight of the tour. Let's move on."

"This is all because Jack Frost and his goblins have the Sweet Fairies' charms!" Rachel whispered.

Kirsty nodded in agreement as Matt ushered them out of the tasting room.

"So here we are in the *Candy Land* factory," Matt announced. Everyone looked around with interest. The sugary smell was even stronger now, and Rachel and Kirsty could see lots of shiny silver machines working away, making different sweets and chocolates. They were operated by workers in spotless white aprons and hats like Matt's.

"This is where the chocolates are packed," Matt went on. He led the group over to a conveyor belt where chocolates wrapped in brightly coloured foil were moving slowly along. A young woman was carefully packing them into gift boxes. "Meet Suzy," Matt said with a grin. "She's the fastest packer in the factory!"

"Hello, everyone." Suzy smiled as she popped the last chocolate into the gift box she was holding, closed it and put it aside. Immediately she began filling an empty box, not allowing a single chocolate on the conveyor belt to get past her.

"See what I mean?" Matt said, and everyone laughed.

"The foil wrappers look very pretty, but the chocolates will taste horrid, thanks to Jack Frost!" Kirsty murmured to Rachel.

Rachel was about to reply when one of the wrappers moving towards them on the conveyor belt caught her attention.

The wrapper was surrounded by a faint, misty, golden glow. As Rachel stared more closely, her heart skipped a beat.

"Kirsty, *that's* not a chocolate wrapper!" she whispered, pointing at the conveyor belt. "It's Clara the Chocolate Fairy!"

Storeroom Surprise

Surprised, Kirsty stared at the conveyor belt and saw the tiny fairy, dressed in a pretty purple dress with a swishy hem and cropped silver leggings. Clara was waving frantically at them.

"Clara's getting closer to where Suzy's packing the gift boxes!" Kirsty said with a worried frown. "If she flies away now, Suzy will see her—"

"And if she stays on the conveyor belt, Clara will end up in a box of chocolates!" Rachel added. "Kirsty, we *have* to help her."

"I'll try and distract Suzy," Kirsty decided. The rest of the group were gathered around, watching Suzy pack the chocolates, and Kirsty hurried to join them.

"Could you tell us what all the different flavours are, Suzy?" Kirsty asked.

"Yes, of course," Suzy replied. She turned away from the conveyor belt a little to glance at Kirsty.

"We have raspberry ripple, strawberry and vanilla creams, caramel and peanut—"

Her long blonde hair streaming behind her, Clara fluttered up from the conveyor belt while Suzy wasn't looking and slipped inside Rachel's shoulder bag.

"Thank you, girls," Clara gushed when Kirsty rejoined them. "I thought I was going to be packed away inside a gift box. I'm here because Jack Frost and his goblins are somewhere in *Candy Land* – and they have my cocoa bean charm!"

"Come along, you two," Matt called to Rachel and Kirsty as the rest of the tour group moved on. 'We're going to look at a giant vat of liquid chocolate!"

"We'll try to get your charm back, Clara," Kirsty promised. "Chocolate tastes really horrible without it!"

Matt and the rest of the group were already gathered around the huge vat of swirling, molten milk chocolate. Clara ducked out of sight as Kirsty and Rachel went to look, too.

"When the chocolate is liquid like this, it can be poured into different-shaped moulds to set," Matt was explaining. "And then—"

Before Matt could finish, the liquid chocolate suddenly began to flow over the sides of the vat. It splashed to the floor, just missing Matt's shoes.

"Oh dear!"
Matt exclaimed,
motioning
for the tour
group
to move
back,
"I don't
know why
everything's
going wrong
today!" He jumped

aside as more chocolate spilled over onto
the floor.

"Could someone sort this out, please?"
Matt called across the room. He turned
back to the tour group. "Let's go, and
I'll show you our chocolate moulds."

Matt escorted the group across the factory to look at the moulds. There were lots of different shapes – hearts, stars, diamonds and eggs – but Rachel and Kirsty were dismayed to see that the moulds were all cracked and bent out of shape.

"I'm *so* sorry, everyone," Matt muttered, looking very embarrassed.

"Poor Matt," Clara whispered to the girls as Matt quickly led them away again. "This isn't his fault – it's because Jack Frost has my cocoa bean charm!"

Kirsty glanced around curiously as

Matt took them over to another corner of the factory. There she saw a huge silver machine squirting chocolate over rows and rows of sticky toffee bars.

"Oh, the machine is making Sticky Toffo Chocs!" Kirsty exclaimed, thrilled.

"That's right," Matt agreed. "And everything seems to be running smoothly here, thank goodness!"

Next to the machine Rachel noticed a factory worker. He was wearing the same white apron and hat as the others, and he was eating a Sticky Toffo Choc with great enjoyment.

"Looks like this batch of chocolates tastes okay," Rachel murmured to Kirsty, "Not like the one you had!"

Matt was frowning at the worker.

"You know, you shouldn't  be eating on the factory floor!" he scolded. "It's against the rules."

"I'm a new taste-tester," the worker mumbled through a mouthful of chocolate and toffee, turning away hastily.

As Matt began telling the group about the machine, Rachel watched as the worker hurried over to a trolley piled

with chocolates. He rushed off with the
trolley, but he was going much too fast.
Suddenly he tripped on the hem of his
long apron and went head over heels.
Rachel gasped as she saw a big pair of
green feet sticking out from beneath the
apron.

"That worker's a goblin!" Rachel
whispered excitedly to Kirsty and Clara.

"Then we have no time to waste!"
declared Clara. "He must have my
cocoa bean charm. Quickly, girls, let me
turn you into fairies before we lose him."

Their hearts pounding, Kirsty and
Rachel slipped out of sight behind the
big silver machine. A cloud of dazzling
sparkles from
Clara's wand
immediately
shrank
the girls
down to
fairy-size
and then,
fluttering their
wings, the three
friends whizzed up into the air.

"There he goes!" Kirsty said, pointing
at the goblin racing across the factory
with the trolley.

"Stay high up so that no one sees us,
girls," Clara told them.

Rachel, Kirsty and Clara zoomed across the factory, keeping the goblin in their sights. They saw him hurry down a corridor, pushing the trolley ahead of him, and then stop by a large metal door marked STOREROOM.

Clara and the girls watched as the goblin heaved the door open.

"He's going inside," Rachel whispered. "We must follow him," said Clara urgently.

The goblin trundled his trolley through
the open door and then let it close
behind him. Rachel, Kirsty and Clara
just managed to fly through before it
banged shut. They perched above the
door and stared around the storeroom.

An extraordinary sight met their eyes.
The storeroom was filled with all kinds
of chocolates. There were heaps of foil-
wrapped gift chocolates on the floor with
the empty boxes tossed into a corner.

There were piles of chocolates in different shapes – hearts and stars and lots of others – on the floor, along with stacks of chocolate bars.

And in the middle of the room, sitting on a heap of Sticky Toffo Chocs and giggling with glee, was Jack Frost himself!

At the Candy Castle

"Give me the magic cocoa bean charm!" Jack Frost demanded, glaring at the goblin worker.

Clara glanced at Rachel and Kirsty in dismay as Jack Frost snatched the charm from the goblin. Jack Frost hung it around his neck, holding the charm up so that it caught the light and sparkled with fairy magic.

"How are we going to get my charm back *now*?" Clara murmured, biting her lip anxiously. She looked so distressed that Kirsty and Rachel felt that they had to do something. Glancing at each other, they swooped down together towards Jack Frost.

"Fairies!" yelled the goblin, pointing at them. Meanwhile, Jack Frost scowled, hiding the cocoa bean charm around his neck with one icy hand.

"What do *you* want?" he sneered.

"You know, you have lots of chocolate here, and it's greedy to keep it for yourself," Kirsty began. "You're causing havoc at *Candy Land,* too!"

"Clara needs her magic charm so that things can get back to normal," added Rachel.

Jack Frost cackled loudly. "I don't care about *Candy Land* and I don't care about silly fairies!" he retorted. "I need heaps of chocolates for my Candy Castle!" Quickly he waved his wand and conjured up a bolt of icy magic. Instantly Jack Frost, his goblin helper and all the chocolate in the storeroom vanished, leaving Clara and the girls alone in an empty room.

"They've taken all the chocolates to the Candy Castle!" Clara gasped. "Let's go, girls!"

This time it was Clara who waved
her wand. Her fairy magic whirled all
three of them off to Fairyland. A few
moments later they were fluttering above
the chocolate wafer drawbridge in front
of the Candy Castle. Because they were
small they could fly unseen by the goblins!

"The castle's getting bigger!" Rachel
exclaimed, staring up at it. "That's why
Jack Frost needs more and more sweets."

Kirsty was frowning. "See those holes
in the cookie walls?" she remarked. "And
some of the brightly coloured gumdrop
decorations are missing."

Clara was looking around the castle
gardens. "The chocolate statue of Jack
Frost has only got one hand, and some of
Lottie the Lollipop Fairy's lollipop flowers
are missing!" she announced. "Just the

sticks are left in the ground."

Clara, Rachel and Kirsty flew along the drawbridge to the enormous chocolate door that led into the castle. Jack Frost was standing in front of the door, yelling at a group of goblin builders. As Clara and the girls got closer, they could see that a big bite had been taken right out of the middle of the door.

"You fools!" Jack Frost was shouting furiously. "You're supposed to be *building* my castle, not *eating* it!"

Clara, Rachel and Kirsty glanced at each other. They couldn't help smiling. They all knew how greedy the goblins could be!

"No more snacking on my sweeties!" Jack Frost ordered the goblins, fixing them with a cold stare. "I want my castle finished *immediately*!"

As Jack Frost continued to rant, Kirsty noticed a goblin crouching in the shadow of the chocolate door. She could see he was chewing away at the strawberry laces holding up the chocolate wafer drawbridge. Kirsty nudged Rachel and Clara to warn them, and the three of them fluttered safely up into the air. Jack

Frost spotted them and shook his fist in their direction.

"Pesky fairies!" he roared. "You'll *never* get the magical cocoa bean charm away from me!" And as the drawbridge crashed into the milkshake moat with a loud splash, Jack Frost dashed inside the Candy Castle.

Messy Mosaic

"Come on, girls!" Clara cried, and she, Rachel and Kirsty flew into the castle after Jack Frost. He began dodging in and out of different rooms, trying to get away from them, but Clara and the girls could easily follow because they could hear him yelling at the greedy goblins as he ran by.

"Stop eating my drawing room!" Jack Frost shouted at some goblins munching on a table and chairs made from mint chocolate wafers. With Clara, Rachel and Kirsty close behind, he rushed through the Great Hall where a goblin was nibbling at a picture frame made of golden honeycomb.

"Soon there'll be no Candy Castle left!" Jack Frost wailed. He gave a yelp of rage as he ran past another room. "Don't eat my ice cream!" he shouted angrily. Kirsty peeked into the bathroom as she, Clara and Rachel flew past, and she saw a goblin spooning dollops of Esme the Ice Cream Fairy's green ice cream from the tub.

Jack Frost dashed up the winding staircase where a goblin was munching away on the cookie steps and then turned down a chocolate-panelled corridor. Clara, Rachel and Kirsty zoomed after him and saw that the corridor was a dead end.

"We've got him cornered, girls!" Clara sighed with relief.

But Jack Frost glared at them and pressed a white chocolate button on one of the panels. A secret door slid back and Jack Frost smiled smugly.

"Goodbye, foolish fairies!" he shouted. But when he rushed through the door, instead of closing it behind him, Jack Frost stopped dead and let out a shriek of horror. "Oh no! My candy bedroom is ruined!" he wailed. "*Ruined!*"

Clara, Rachel and Kirsty flew into the room behind him. They saw an enormous bed made of soft marshmallow with bites taken out of it. The furniture was made of dark chocolate and some of the drawers and doorknobs were missing. On the bedside table, Rachel saw the throne decoration from Coco the Cupcake Fairy, but all that was left of the cupcake it was on were a few crumbs.

Jack Frost was gazing at the floor, sniffling tearfully to himself.

"Why is he so upset about the floor?" Kirsty wondered, staring down at it. The floor was made of tiles in white, milk and dark chocolate, but some of them had obviously been nibbled away. Kirsty peered at it a little more closely and finally realised 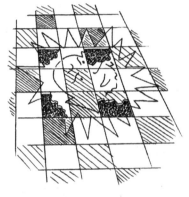 what she was looking at – the floor had been a mosaic portrait of Jack Frost himself before some of the tiles had been gobbled up by the goblins, including Jack Frost's nose! She quickly pointed this out to Clara and Rachel as Jack Frost sobbed.

53

"My beautiful floor!" Jack Frost groaned, icy tears dripping down his face. "It was a wonderful work of chocolate art."

Rachel fluttered forward. "Clara can help you fix the missing tiles," she pointed out, "*if* you give her magic charm back."

"Of course I'm not giving it back!" Jack Frost snapped. "Can't you see I need the chocolate magic of the cocoa bean charm more than ever now?" And he pointed at the ruined floor.

Kirsty stared down at the chocolate tiles. Suddenly a picture of her own favourite chocolate, the Sticky Toffo Choc, popped into her head. That gave her an idea!

A Sticky Situation!

Kirsty turned to Clara and Rachel and whispered her plan to them.

Clara smiled. "I know a fairy who can help you," she told Jack Frost.

The girls watched as Clara waved her wand, writing a glittering word in the air – *Lizzie*. Then, a second or two later, Lizzie the Sweet Treats Fairy appeared in a cloud of magical sparkles.

"Hello,
everyone!"
Lizzie cried.
"Hello,
Lizzie," Kirsty
and Rachel
said together,
beaming at
their old friend.
Lizzie was one of the
Princess Fairies.

Jack Frost groaned loudly. "More
fairies!" he muttered. "Go away and
leave me alone!"

"Lizzie's going to make your mosaic
chocolate floor even better than it was
before," Rachel told him. She murmured
something in a low voice to Lizzie who
smiled and nodded.

"Hurry up, then!" Jack Frost said rudely.

Lizzie waved her wand around her head.

Sparkling fairy dust flew from the wand to the four corners of the room, floating softly down onto the

ruined tiles. In a flash, the missing tiles were instantly replaced. The floor looked as good as new, complete with a mosaic picture of Jack Frost's face.

"Hurrah!" Jack Frost yelled excitedly, "My chocolate floor is wonderful again!

And don't I look handsome?" Proudly
he tried to rush forward to get a better
look at his giant portrait, but his feet
just wouldn't move. Rachel and Kirsty
grinned at each other.

"What's going on?" Jack Frost roared
angrily. "I'm stuck! My feet are stuck
to the floor!" He bent over and stared
at the tiles more closely. Then
he gave another scream
of rage. "These tiles
aren't chocolate –
they're *toffee*!"

Furious,
Jack Frost
hit out at
the four fairies
hovering above him,
but they simply flew out of his reach.

Jack Frost tried to stomp his feet in a rage, but he couldn't because he was stuck fast to the toffee. Rachel fluttered over to him. Dodging Jack Frost's flailing arms, she managed to unhook the cocoa bean charm from his necklace.

"I think this belongs to someone else!" Rachel said, shaking her head at him.

"Give it back!" Jack Frost demanded, but Rachel ignored him and flew over to Clara.

Clara smiled joyfully when Rachel
handed her the glowing magical charm,
which became fairy-sized the instant
Clara touched it.

"Thank you,
girls, and thank
you, Lizzie,
for all your
help!" Clara
declared,
clasping the
magic cocoa
bean tightly.
"Now Lizzie
and I must return to

Fairyland and share the good news with
everyone."

"But we can't leave Jack Frost stuck in
the toffee, can we?" Kirsty pointed out.

"Oops, I almost forgot!" Clara gasped. With one flick of her wand, her magic turned the toffee tiles back to chocolate. Jack Frost stopped yelling with fury and looked thrilled instead.

"My beautiful floor is back!" he exclaimed, dancing around with glee. "And the chocolate me looks marvellous!"

Rachel, Kirsty, Clara and Lizzie laughed.

"But that's *all* the chocolate you're getting!" Kirsty warned Jack Frost as he continued to jig happily around the room. Then, with a flick of Clara's wand, her fairy magic whisked Rachel and Kirsty back to *Candy Land*.

Chocolates are Magic!

Almost instantly the girls found themselves in the *Candy Land* factory again and once more restored to their normal human size. Quickly, they hurried out from behind the Sticky Toffo Choc machine to join the rest of the group. Kirsty was relieved to see that no one seemed to have noticed they had been missing.

"And now we're going to take a look at where we keep our chocolates before they're sent out to the sweet shops," Matt was saying. "Follow me, everyone."

Matt led the way across the factory floor and down a corridor. The girls exchanged anxious glances.

"This is the way we chased the goblin with the trolley," Rachel whispered to Kirsty. "Matt's taking us to the storeroom."

"But we know the storeroom's empty!" Kirsty said, looking very worried. "Jack Frost took all the chocolates for his Candy Castle. What's Matt going to say when he sees there's nothing there?"

"Here we are." Matt stopped outside the door marked STOREROOM. The girls held their breath as he swung the door open.

To Rachel and Kirsty's delight, they could see that the room was once again full of chocolate. But this time the gift boxes were arranged in neat piles, the chocolate bars were stacked tidily, and there were no heaps of chocolates on the floor.

"Clara must have returned it all with her magic," Rachel murmured happily, "And she's tidied up all that mess Jack Frost and his goblin made, too."

"And look, she even left us some more samples to try!" Kirsty said, pointing at a tray of chocolates sitting on a table.

Matt was staring at the samples, looking very surprised. "Well, we usually lay out all our samples in the tasting room," he said with a smile. "But let's try these ones, too."

Kirsty chose another Sticky Toffo Choc and so did Rachel. This time the chocolates tasted utterly delicious.

"Mmm!" was all Rachel could say for a moment or two as she enjoyed the combination of delicious milky chocolate and sticky toffee. The rest of the tour group were also ooh-ing and aah-ing in delight as they ate their samples. Even

Matt selected a Sticky Toffo Choc and popped it in his mouth.

"Absolutely magic!" he said.

Rachel and Kirsty grinned at each other.

Rachel laughed. "That's exactly what I think!" she said.

After the tour the girls thanked Matt and then hurried to join Aunt Harri in the canteen. She was sitting at a table, waiting for them.

"I hope you've had a good time, girls," Aunt Harri said with a smile. "And I hope you're not *too* sick of chocolate because there's chocolate cake for dessert!"

"Yum!" Kirsty said, "We'd never get sick of chocolate, would we, Rachel?"

"No way!" Rachel agreed. "And we're having a great time."

"Well, I hope you'll have fun this afternoon with me in the cookie department," Aunt Harri said. "Now, let's go up to the counter and order our lunch."

Rachel and Kirsty glanced meaningfully at each other as they followed Aunt Harri to the canteen counter. Treat Day was getting closer and closer,

and, although they'd returned four of the Sweet Fairies' magic charms, there were still three left to find. Would they manage to get them back before Treat Day was ruined for everyone in Fairyland? Or would they run out of time?

**Now it's time for Kirsty and
Rachel to help...**

Madeleine the Cookie Fairy

Read on for a sneak peek...

The yellow walls of the *Candy Land* sweet factory were gleaming in the midday sun, and the brightly coloured flags on its roof waved in the spring breeze. In the factory café, Rachel Walker and Kirsty Tate were finishing their sandwiches and chatting to Kirsty's Aunt Harri.

"You're so lucky to work here," Rachel said. "It's my dream job!"

"You wouldn't say that if you could see all the paperwork I have to do," replied Aunt Harri with a laugh.

"Yes, but you get to taste all the new

sweets," said Kirsty with a giggle. "That sounds like the best job in the world!"

Aunt Harri laughed and glanced up at the clock on the wall.

"It does mean I could organise a tour of the factory for my favourite niece and her best friend!" she said with a smile. "Have you enjoyed the tour so far?"

It was Kirsty's birthday tomorrow, and this special day at *Candy Land* was an early birthday treat. Because Rachel was staying with Kirsty over half term, she had been given a ticket too.

"It's been brilliant!" said Rachel. "The chocolate department was amazing."

"Yes, thank you for the tickets, Aunt Harri," said Kirsty. "Today is one of the best birthday presents I've ever had!"

"It's not over yet," said Aunt Harri

with a grin. "You'll be spending this afternoon with me in the cookie department. But first I've got another little treat for you. Wait here and I'll be right back."

She winked at them and headed into the café. Rachel and Kirsty looked at each other with shining eyes.

"I don't know how this day could get any better!" said Rachel. "Isn't this perfect?"

Read Madeleine the Cookie Fairy to find out what adventures are in store for Kirsty and Rachel!

Meet the Sweet Fairies

If Kirsty and Rachel don't find
the Sweet Fairies' magical charms,
Jack Frost will ruin all sweet treats for ever!

www.rainbowmagicbooks.co.uk

Meet the fairies, play games
and get sneak peeks at
the latest books!

www.rainbowmagicbooks.co.uk

There's fairy fun for everyone on
our wonderful website.
You'll find great activities, competitions, stories and
fairy profiles, and also a special newsletter.

Get 30% off all Rainbow Magic books at

www.rainbowmagicbooks.co.uk

Enter the code RAINBOW at the checkout.
Offer ends 31 December 2013.

Offer valid in United Kingdom and Republic of Ireland only.

Competition!

The Sweet Fairies have created a special competition just for you!
In the back of each book in the Sweet Fairies series there will
be a question for you to answer. First you need to collect the
answer from the back of each book in the series.
Once you have all the answers, take the first letter from each one
and arrange them to spell a secret word!
When you have the answer, go online and enter!

We will put all the correct entries into a draw and select a winner
to receive a special Rainbow Magic Goodie Bag featuring lots of
treats for you and your fairy friends. You'll also star in a new
Rainbow Magic story!

Which Rainbow Magic Fairy is the Easter Fairy?

Enter online now at www.rainbowmagicbooks.co.uk

Nicki the Holiday Camp Fairy

Rachel and Kirsty have been looking forward to camp, but everything is going wrong. Can they help Nicki fix things, before the whole summer is ruined?

www.rainbowmagicbooks.co.uk